Ladybird  Readers

Dash and Thud

Series Editor: Sorrel Pitts
Story by Catherine Baker
Illustrated by Ian Cunliffe

Ladybird Readers Starter Level

Title		Phonics	Sight Words
1	Alphabet Book	A—Z	
2	Is it Nat?	s a t p i n	a is it
3	Nat Sits		an in sit
4	Top Dog and Pompom	m d g o c k	and can I into no
5	Top Dog is Sick		got not
6	The Fun Run	e u r h b f l	at get go has off the to up
7	Gus is Hot!		full his of on put
8	Jazz the Vet	j v w x y z qu	be but had he him she tell was
9	Vick the Vet		did well will
10	Dash and Thud	ch sh th ng	if ran then they with yes
11	Big Bad Bash		big long that this
12	The Big Fish	ai ee oa oo	her look see them
13	The Big Ship		let me my too
14	Martin and Lorna	ar or ur ow oi er	all are for
15	Farmer Carl		cut down good help now
16	The Big Dipper	igh ear air ure	as have like said some went you
17	The Silver Ring		come from so stop we what

First, go through the phonemes on page 4, and do the activity on page 5. Then, read the words in the first half of the book, focusing on pronunciation and blending.

The sight words are introduced in the second half of the book, first on their own and then in full sentences.

At the back of the book, there are activities and assessments practicing phonemes and sight words. These icons indicate the key skills required in each activity:

 Spelling and writing   Speaking   Reading

Ladybird Readers

Dash and Thud

Look at the story

First, look at the words and pictures.
Use the words to practice phonics.

Phonics focus

ch   sh   th   ng

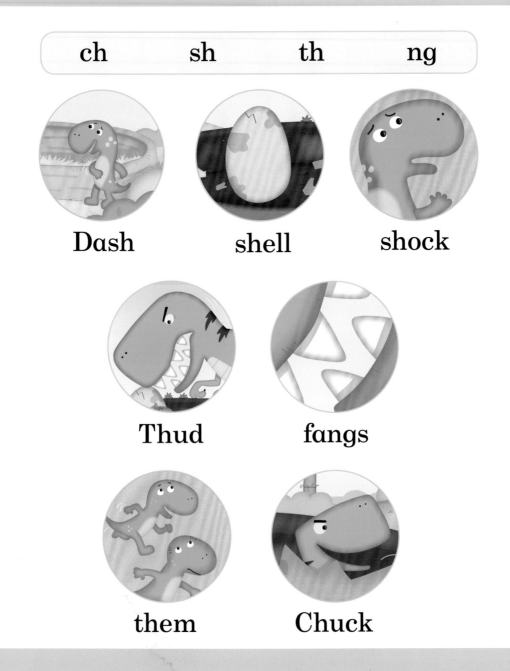

Dash   shell   shock

Thud   fangs

them   Chuck

Aa Bb Cc Dd Ee Ff Gg Hh Ii Jj Kk Ll Mm

Activity

1 Say the sounds. Say the words. Color in the eggs. 🗨️ 📖

ch   ng   sh

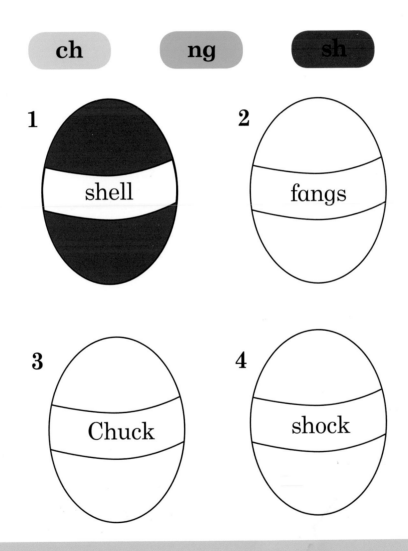

1 shell

2 fangs

3 Chuck

4 shock

Dash

shell

Chuck

9

shock

Thud

fangs

11

Thud

Dash

13

Dash

them

Dash and Thud

Read the story

Now, read the story in full sentences.
Practice using the sight words.

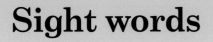

Sight words

if

ran

then

they

with

yes

Meg was not in the den.

Meg was in a big den with a lot of eggshells.

That is a big chick, Dash.

Thud!
Bash!

21

Then, they got a shock.

Run, Meg!
Go back to
Mom.

23

Meg shot off.
Dash ran in a ring.

If I run in rings, I will get ill.

Bang! Thud fell
with a thump.

Meg and Dash got back
to the den.

That was such
a shock!

Mom had a hug with them.

Dash is fab!

Activities

2 Say the sounds and read the
sentences. Write the letters. 🔘📖✏️

short
th
the
Then

long
th
Thud
thump

1 "Thud has big fangs!"

2 Dash got back to
.............e den.

3 Thud fell with a
.............ump.

4 ....en, they got a
shock.

28

3 **Say the words. Draw the pictures.**

Dash ran with Meg.

Then, Thud fell with a thump.

Assessment

4 **Match the words with the same sound.**

1 shell   Thud

2 thing   then

3 ring   shock

4 that   bang

5 Say the sight words.
Write them on the lines.

Yes   with   Then

they   ran   If

1   Thud fell _with_ a thump.

2   _____, they got a shock.

3   "_____, Mom. I will be quick."

4   Dash _____ in a ring.

5   "_____ I run in rings, I will get ill."

6   Then, _____ got a shock.

Starter

Ladybird Readers — Starter 1 — **Alphabet Book**	Ladybird Readers — Starter 2 — **Is it Nat?**	Ladybird Readers — Starter 3 — **Nat Sits**	Ladybird Readers — Starter 4 — **Top Dog and Pompom**	Ladybird Readers — Starter 5 — **Top Dog is Sick**
978-0-241-39367-3 ☐	978-0-241-39368-0 ☐	978-0-241-39369-7 ☐	978-0-241-39370-3 ☐	978-0-241-39371-0 ☐
Ladybird Readers — Starter 6 — **The Fun Run**	Ladybird Readers — Starter 7 — **Gus is Hot!**	Ladybird Readers — Starter 8 — **Jazz the Vet**	Ladybird Readers — Starter 9 — **Vick the Vet**	Ladybird Readers — Starter 10 — **Dash and Thud**
978-0-241-39372-7 ☐	978-0-241-39373-4 ☐	978-0-241-39374-1 ☐	978-0-241-39375-8 ☐	978-0-241-39376-5 ☐
Ladybird Readers — Starter 11 — **Big Bad Bash**	Ladybird Readers — Starter 12 — **The Big Fish**	Ladybird Readers — Starter 13 — **The Big Ship**	Ladybird Readers — Starter 14 — **Martin and Lorna**	Ladybird Readers — Starter 15 — **Farmer Carl**
978-0-241-39377-2 ☐	978-0-241-39379-6 ☐	978-0-241-39380-2 ☐	978-0-241-39381-9 ☐	978-0-241-39382-6 ☐
Ladybird Readers — Starter 16 — **The Big Dipper**	Ladybird Readers — Starter 17 — **The Silver Ring**			
978-0-241-39383-3 ☐	978-0-241-39384-0 ☐			

LADYBIRD BOOKS

UK | USA | Canada | Ireland | Australia
India | New Zealand | South Africa

Ladybird Books is part of the Penguin Random House group of companies
whose addresses can be found at global.penguinrandomhouse.com.
www.penguin.co.uk   www.puffin.co.uk   www.ladybird.co.uk

Penguin
Random House
UK

First published 2017. This edition published 2019
001

Copyright © Ladybird Books Ltd, 2017

Printed in China

A CIP catalogue record for this book is available from the British Library

ISBN: 978-0-241-39376-5

All correspondence to:
Ladybird Books
Penguin Random House Children's
80 Strand, London WC2R 0RL